SO YOU WANNA BE

A Dancer

SANDRA K. ATHANS

Rourke Educational Media
rourkeeducationalmedia.com

Before & After Reading Activities

Before Reading:

Building Academic Vocabulary and Background Knowledge

Before reading a book, it is important to tap into what your child or students already know about the topic. This will help them develop their vocabulary, increase their reading comprehension, and make connections across the curriculum.

1. *Look at the cover of the book. What will this book be about?*
2. *What do you already know about the topic?*
3. *Let's study the Table of Contents. What will you learn about in the book's chapters?*
4. *What would you like to learn about this topic? Do you think you might learn about it from this book? Why or why not?*
5. *Use a reading journal to write about your knowledge of this topic. Record what you already know about the topic and what you hope to learn about the topic.*
6. *Read the book.*
7. *In your reading journal, record what you learned about the topic and your response to the book.*
8. *After reading the book complete the activities below.*

Content Area Vocabulary

Read the list. What do these words mean?

advanced degree
agents
auditions
capitals
certificate
choreographers
conservatory
finance
journalist
marketing
operas
professional
props

After Reading:

Comprehension and Extension Activity

After reading the book, work on the following questions with your child or students in order to check their level of reading comprehension and content mastery.

1. *What types of careers are available for dancers? (Summarize)*
2. *Why do dancers learn many different styles of dance? (Infer)*
3. *What role do agents play in helping dancers build their careers? (Asking Questions)*
4. *Which careers interest you the most? (Text to Self Connection)*
5. *How do many young dancers improve their skill and build their dance knowledge as they get older? (Asking Questions)*

Extension Activity

Pick a dance career that interests you the most. Make a visual timeline plan that will help you achieve your career goals. Begin by listing those actions you can take now. Then, add the steps you will take in two years, in four years, and then finally in six or more years. Add visuals such as photographs, articles, or tickets to performances you attend to illustrate your goals and ideas. Keep this plan and update it regularly to document your progress and growth.

Table of Contents

Becoming a Professional

If you love to dance, then you'll leap in your leotard over the many kinds of jobs that await you!

GET STARTED!

1. Get to know yourself as a dancer—your strengths, interests, and ambitions.
2. Keep a journal to track your progress, accomplishments, and challenges.

There are dream jobs such as joining a **professional** ballet company or dancing on stage with the trending boy band. There are lesser-known jobs too, such as dance therapy.

PRO ADVICE

"NO DANCER EVER BECAME SUCCESSFUL RIDING ON THEIR NATURAL BORN TALENTS ONLY. DANCERS ARE ARTISTS AND ATHLETES. THE WORLD OF DANCE TODAY IS AKIN TO AN EXTREME SPORT. NATURAL ABILITY AND TALENT WILL ONLY GET US SO FAR. DANCERS MUST WORK HARD AND PERSEVERE. DANCERS GIVE YEARS OF THEIR LIVES PLUS THEIR SWEAT, TEARS AND SOMETIMES BLOOD TO HAVE THE HONOR AND PLEASURE OF PERFORMING ON STAGE."

—MELANIE DOSKOCIL, DIRECTOR OF THE SCHOOL OF ASPEN SANTA FE BALLET WITH MORE THAN 20 YEARS OF PROFESSIONAL DANCE AND TEACHING EXPERIENCE

Professional dancers perform in ballets, **operas**, musical theater, and more. Not surprisingly, there are more dancers than there are dance jobs. This makes the competition fierce! The good news is there are many other jobs that can fuel a dancer's passion.

Dancers often begin taking dance classes at an early age. They study ballet, tap, jazz, and other styles. Later, they may attend special dance schools, such as a performing arts college or a **conservatory**. Many hope to join a professional dance company.

Dancers who add singing and acting to their performance skills open doors to more opportunities in musical theater.

Opportunities for people with disabilities to dance continue to grow, showcasing the talents of these skilled dancers.

FAST FACT

Students pursuing dance careers may study at a college or university that offers an **advanced degree** in dance. They might also attend specialty dance schools or conservatories. Select students may be invited to join a professional dance company. These are traditional paths to dance success. But some students continue their studies on their own. They may join a dance studio, view online videos, or take part in classes offered through community programs.

Entertainment Dancers

Entertainment dancers perform on cruise lines and in theme parks.

Some cities, such as Las Vegas and New York City, are known as entertainment **capitals**. Spectacular dance and theatrical acts perform there year-round.

The Rockettes are precision dancers known for their eye-high kicks. They perform at Radio City Music Hall in New York City. Their form of precision dance blends ballet, jazz, tap, and modern dance styles.

Auditions and Agents

Most dancers try out for dance jobs at **auditions.** Dancers learn about auditions through postings in online dance publications or dance platforms such as *Backstage* and *BroadwayWorld*.

Agents are another source of audition news. They can suggest auditions that match your interests, work out fees and conditions for your work, and help you make connections to advance your career. Dancers must often build experience on their own before they can get an agent. Some dancers may choose to become agents themselves!

PRO ADVICE

"MY ADVICE IS TO TRAIN LIKE YOU'VE NEVER TRAINED BEFORE! ALSO, DON'T EVER GIVE UP! I REMEMBER SEEING AN AMERICAN IN PARIS WHEN IT FIRST OPENED AND THEN AUDITIONING FOR THE BROADWAY PRODUCTION EIGHT TIMES BEFORE THEY TOLD ME I WAS IN AND WOULD START REHEARSALS NEXT WEEK. IT WAS MY SHOW, AND I WAS GOING TO FIGHT FOR IT!"

—ALEX AQUILINO, BROADWAY PERFORMER

Backup Commercial Dancers

Commercial dance is high-energy support dance. Dancers may back up live stage performers, be extras in a music video, or dance in a product commercial.

Like other professional dance jobs, getting your foot in the door as a commercial dancer often begins at an audition.

Backup dancers perform behind recording artist Camila Cabello during a concert.

PRO ADVICE

"FINDING AN AGENT IS ONE OF THE HARDEST THINGS FOR YOUNG PERFORMERS. MY COLLEGE ARRANGED A SHOWCASE IN NEW YORK CITY WHERE ALL ACTING AND MUSICAL THEATER STUDENTS PERFORMED TO AN AUDIENCE OF OVER 100 AGENTS. FROM THIS, I WAS ABLE TO GET A LIST OF THE ONES WHO WERE INTERESTED IN ME. ALTHOUGH I DIDN'T END UP GETTING AN AGENT FROM THE SHOWCASE, I HAD A LOT OF NAMES AND ADDRESSES. EVERY SIX MONTHS, I WOULD EMAIL AND UPDATE THEM ON WHAT I'D BEEN DOING. I TOLD THEM I WAS STILL SEEKING REPRESENTATION, AND I ALWAYS ASKED TO SET UP A MEETING."

—RYAN MAC, NEW YORK CITY-BASED ACTOR, SINGER, DANCER, AND PIANIST

Choreographers

Choreographers create dance movements, steps, and routines. Projects may range from a hip-hop routine to a ballet performance. These professionals also direct dancers and help them master the steps.

You must have imagination and knowledge of all major dance styles for success in this career!

Breakdancing is a high-energy dance style that blends crisp footwork and flashy floor acrobatics such as spinning on one's knees, hands, or head.

PRO ADVICE

"TODAY'S TECHNOLOGY IS A CHOREOGRAPHER'S BEST TOOL. YOU CAN FILM YOUR DANCES, WATCH THEM BACK, AND GET FEEDBACK FROM OTHERS. LISTENING TO FEEDBACK HELPS YOU DEVELOP AND FIND YOUR OWN DANCE VOICE. TECHNOLOGY ALSO BRINGS YOUR WORK TO THE STAGE. BY USING YOUR OWN PHONE, SPACE, AND ONLINE PLATFORM, ONE MILLION PEOPLE CAN SEE A VIDEO OF YOUR WORK. THIS IS LOW COST EXPOSURE, AND YOU CAN GET IT ON YOUR OWN, WITHOUT AN AGENT OR PRODUCER. TECHNOLOGY OPENS THE DOOR FOR MORE PEOPLE TO GET DISCOVERED!'

—JON ARPINO, CO-FOUNDER AND CEO OF CLI STUDIOS, A COMPANY THAT BRINGS ONLINE CLASSES FROM WORLD-RENOWNED CHOREOGRAPHERS TO DANCE STUDIOS AROUND THE WORLD

NOTATORS

Dance notators use symbols to record dance movements so they are remembered over time. Dancers also use the records to tweak and perfect dance routines. What's new in notation? The use of tiny video cameras attached to dancers' shoes!

Designers

Set and lighting designers help dress a stage using **props**, lighting, sound, and special effects. These careers often require formal education, technical training, and/or a **certificate**.

FAST FACT

Colleges and universities offer programs in costume design. College internship programs place students in design companies where they get real-world experience. Working with local dance studios or community theaters is another option for getting started. Gain experience from the ground up, build a reputation, and then expand beyond your community.

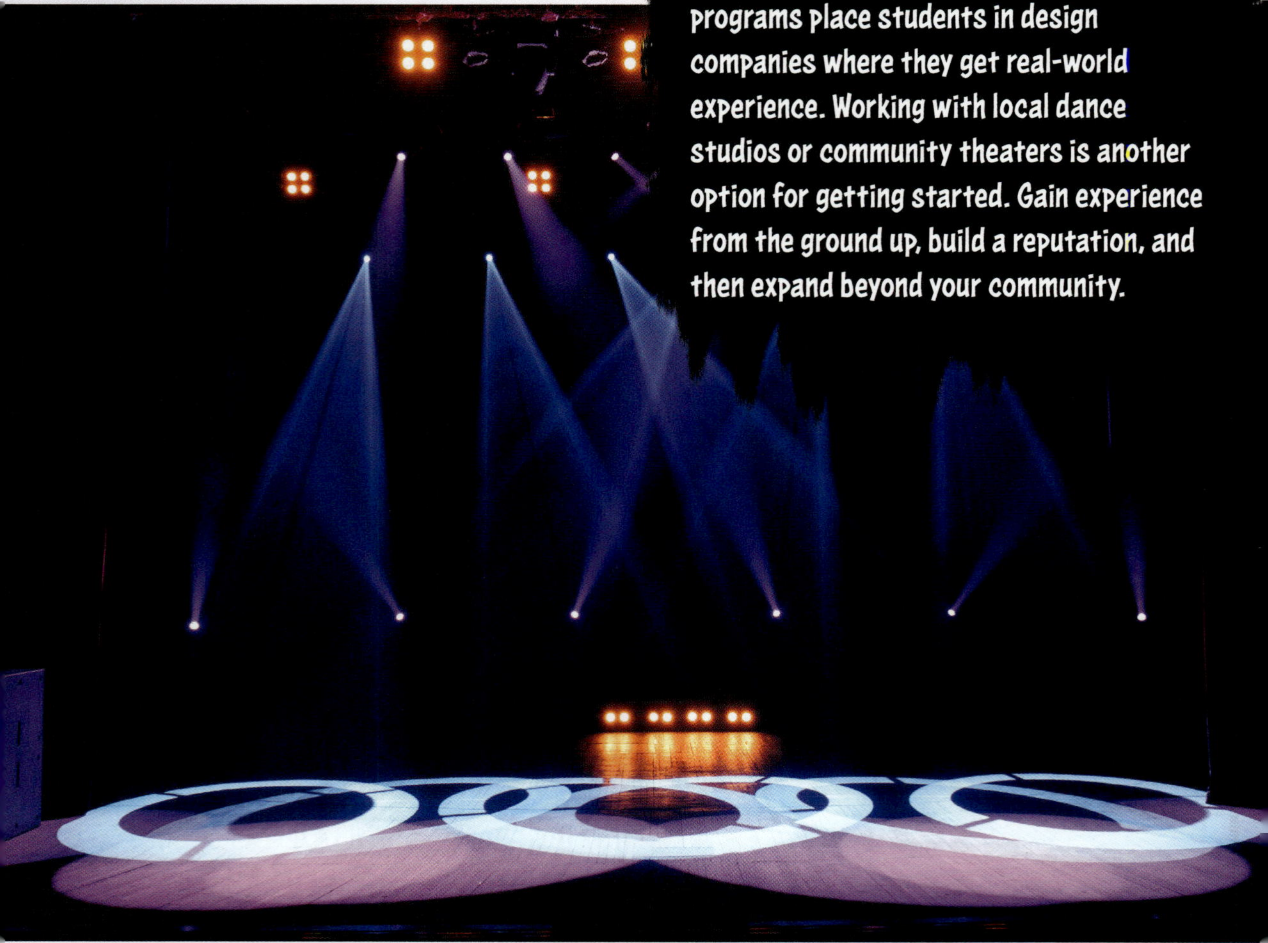

Imaginative lighting, sound, and video invite new interactions between technology and the arts.

Costume designers create eye-popping outfits, from ballroom gowns to fancy footwear. Some design for competitions or recitals. Designers must know fabrics, and how they drape and flow. Costume designers work with directors, choreographers, and dancers to help tell a story.

GET STARTED!

1. Join the backstage crew for school or community events.
2. Keep a special sketchbook to draw props or costume ideas.
3. Stay up to date with fashion trends.

The Business of Dance

Dance administrators focus on **finance** and other matters. They help dance companies make important decisions and plans for the future.

Marketing and public relations specialists contact newspapers, television stations, and social media sites to tell them about important dance news. They also set up interviews and help dancers keep their websites up to date.

FAST FACT

Most companies require that individuals who hold these positions have formal dance and/or business backgrounds as well as excellent speaking, writing, and people skills.

PRO ADVICE

"Dancers who want to own and teach in their own dance studio must understand that the field is very competitive. In addition to going to a college that specializes in dance and business, they can also volunteer in different studios to get an understanding of the many behind-the-scene responsibilities and different instructional styles. They need to develop their creativity and also develop business savvy, such as advertising and finance."

—Kellie Ellis, associate director and dance instructor, Syracuse Children's Theater

Writing About Dance

A dance **journalist** or blogger captures the who, what, when, where, and why of dance. They review performances, hold interviews, and report industry news.

GET STARTED!

1. Help write programs for your school or community dance events.
2. Write articles and reviews for your school newspaper.
3. Read dance journals housed in your school or local library.
4. Start a blog and write about local dance news and performances.

PRO ADVICE

"I WAIT FOR NO ONE! I AM A HUSTLER. I AM A CHASER, ESPECIALLY IN TODAY'S WORLD WHERE YOU ARE ONLY A FEW CLICKS AWAY FROM GETTING IN DIRECT CONTACT WITH PEOPLE WHO MIGHT HAVE USE FOR YOUR CREATIVE TALENTS. THERE'S AN EXPECTATION THAT THE ONES WHO REALLY WANT SUCCESS ARE THE ONES MAKING CONNECTIONS AND BEING BOLD."

—RUTHIE FIERBERG, SENIOR FEATURES EDITOR, *PLAYBILL*

PHOTOGRAPHERS AND VIDEOGRAPHERS

Dance photography and videography are other picture-perfect careers! Both involve capturing sharp visual images of dancers in motion. The photos may be used in dance journals, books, documentaries, calendars, and advertisements. Some are featured in special gallery displays. Dance photographers also help dancers. They provide headshots, business cards, and video clips needed for auditions or websites.

Dance Instructors and Trainers

Do you love working with children? Do you enjoy helping others perfect their dance moves? Are you patient and caring? If so, you might be an excellent dance instructor!

You could teach at a local dance studio, at a school or college, or for your community. You could teach children, teens, or adults.

Many dancers who are members of studio teams or dance companies attend competitions. Judging these competitions or assisting with choreography, costumes, or hair and makeup are other jobs instructors fill.

GET STARTED!

1. Guide younger dancers during team competitions.
2. Help instructors who teach community classes.
3. Assist your physical education teacher with dance fitness activities.

Dance competitions may feature dance teams from around the world, making them exciting opportunities for everyone involved.

Some dancers work as sports trainers. They help athletes build strength and improve their movement. Many dancers coach athletes as part of a training routine.

Dance instructors and trainers often have special training and advanced degrees.

Alex Collins, a running back with the Baltimore Ravens, learned Irish dancing to help his game.

Dance Medicine

Dance medicine specialists help dancers mend after injury. Dancers train and practice cautiously, but strains, sprains, bruising, and foot and ankle injuries happen often.

Dance movement therapists use movement to help improve people's health. They set goals, guide dance sessions, and give advice.

MEDICAL SPECIALISTS

1. Orthopedic Surgeon: treats injuries affecting muscles, bones, and joints.
2. Physical Therapist: uses exercises and other types of care to help improve movement.
3. Nutritionist/Dietician: helps others learn about food and healthy eating habits.
4. Kinesiologist: studies motor skills, movement, and physical activity.

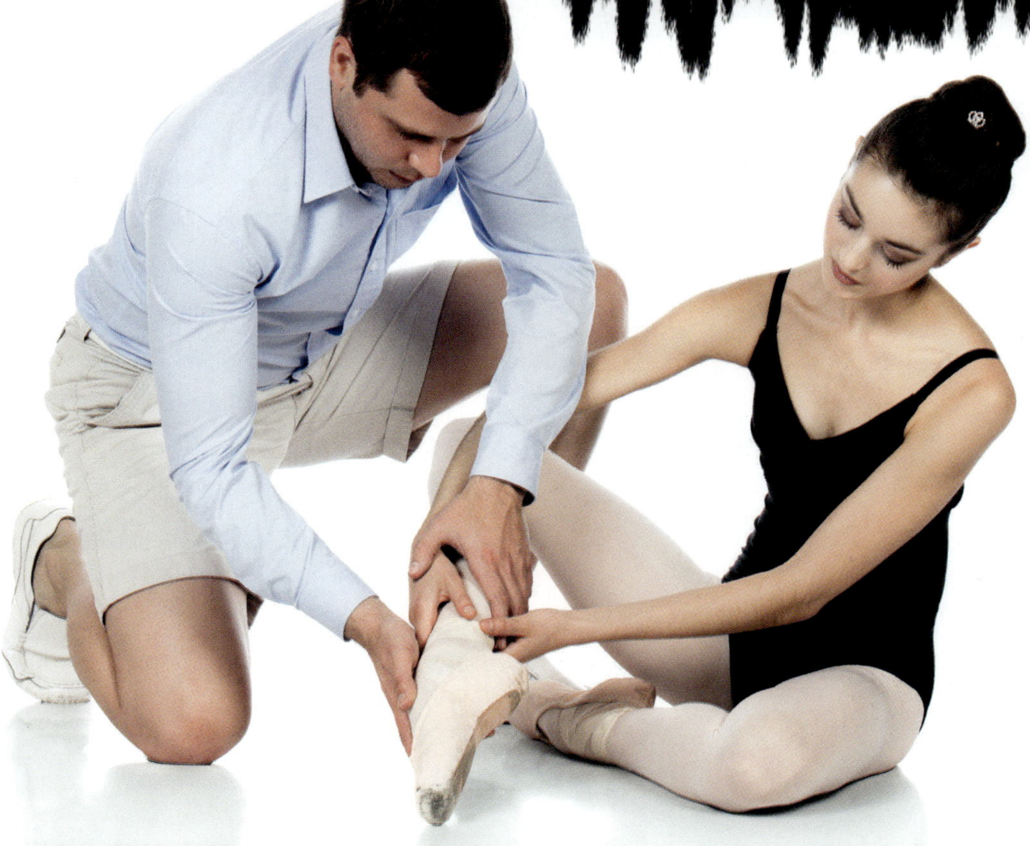

Dancers who want to pursue a medical career may begin at the same time they launch their formal dance. After completing their studies, they may find a good fit in a dance clinic or center within a large medical hospital or university.

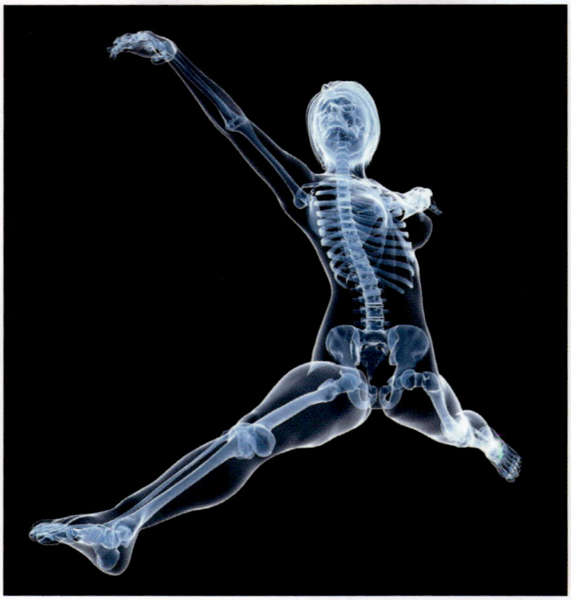

PRO ADVICE

"IF YOU'RE INTERESTED IN DANCE MEDICINE, IT'S IMPORTANT TO HAVE AN END VISION—EVEN THOUGH THIS CAN BE TRICKY! LOOK CAREFULLY AT THE DIFFERENT SPECIALTIES OF DANCE MEDICINE THAT INTEREST YOU. ALSO THINK ABOUT THE TYPE OF EMPLOYMENT THAT WILL SATISFY YOU. THE PROGRAMS ARE VERY COMPETITIVE AND REQUIRE YEARS OF COMMITMENT. DECISIONS YOU MAKE ALONG YOUR PATH CAN AFFECT THE OUTCOME OF YOUR CAREER."

—SARAH REIS, MED, KINESIOLOGY, INTERNATIONAL DANCE TEACHING STANDARDS (IDTS), BRITISH COLUMBIA, CANADA

Sarah Reis taught dance classes while going to school to study kinesiology.

FAST FACT

All medical careers require advanced college degrees, special training, and hands-on experience in clinics or hospitals. Some schools offer degree programs in dance and dance science. Students take classes in nutrition, anatomy, physiology, and psychology. These schools often offer internships, shadowing, research opportunities, and other support for dance students who also want to pursue an advanced medical degree.

The Perfect Hobby

There are many careers for dancers but enjoying dance as a hobby is swell as well!

Attending studio classes or joining a local dance group is one way to keep things simple. Competing in annual dance competitions that take place worldwide is another. You can also explore cultural dancing at community festivals and events.

You can support dance by attending dance performances and following the careers of your favorite dancers. As a patron you can connect with others who share your love of dance!

Serious dancers take charge of their success. They practice regularly and improve their skills by going to school, taking studio classes, or studying videos online.

Dancers who want to be professionals follow the jobs. They know they might have to take many small jobs before they land a big one. They understand that it can be a frustrating business with more struggles than successes to start. But they are willing to do what it takes!

PRO ADVICE

"THE BIGGEST TRAIT YOU NEED IS CONFIDENCE. IF YOU'RE CONFIDENT IN YOURSELF AND IN YOUR STYLE AND ABILITY, YOU CAN HOLD UP TO THE COMPETITION, WHICH CAN BE INTENSE, AND PUSH THROUGH ALL THE UPS AND DOWNS."
—JON ARPINO, CO-FOUNDER AND CEO OF CLI STUDIOS

Glossary

advanced degree (uhd-VANST di-GREE): titles given by a university or college showing a student has completed a higher level of studies

agents (AY-juhnts): people who arrange things for other people

auditions (aw-DISH-uhns): short performances by someone to see whether or not he or she is suitable for a part in a production

capitals (KAP-i-tuhls): places that are well-known for important activities and events

certificate (sur-TIF-uh-kit): a piece of paper that officially states that something is a fact

choreographers (kor-ee-AH-gruh-furs): people who arrange steps and movements for dances

conservatory (kuhn-SUR-vuh-toor-ee): a school that specializes in classes in the arts

finance (FYE-nans): the management and use of money by businesses, banks, and governments

journalist (JUR-nuh-list): someone who writes for newspapers, magazines, television, or radio

marketing (MAHR-ki-ting): the act of promoting and selling products or services

operas (AH-pur-uhs): plays in which all or most of the words are sung and there is an orchestra

professional (pruh-FESH-uh-nuhl): making money for doing something others do for fun

props (prahps): any items other than costumes or furniture that appear on a stage or a movie set

Index

Show What You Know

1. What type of schools do many dance students attend to continue their studies?
2. Why would it be helpful for a choreographer to have professional dance experience?
3. What are some ways to seek out and prepare for an audition?
4. Which careers require excellent speaking, writing, and people skills?
5. What are several things you can do today to launch your future dance career?

Further Reading

Herweck, Dona, *A Day in the Life of a Ballet Dancer*, Time For Kids, 2014.

Various Authors., *Shall We Dance?* Paperback Set of 8: *Ballet, Ballroom Dance, Dance Team, Hip-Hop Dance, Irish Dance, Jazz Dance, Modern Dance, Tap Dance, Focus Readers*, 2017.

Siwa, JoJo, *JoJo's Guide to the Sweet Life: #PeaceOutHaterz*, Harry N. Abrams, 2017.

About the Author

Meet The Author!
www.meetREMauthors.com

Sandra K. Athans is a former dance event planner for a children's summer camp. She is also a writer, a teacher, and a part-time "dance mom" for her students. Many of her students wanna be dancers! They love to share stories of their dance experiences, like their nervous jitters before a competition or their high-spirited relief after nailing a tricky routine! All dancers have an exciting story to tell! What's yours?

www.rourkeeducationalmedia.com

PHOTO CREDITS: Cover & Title Pg ©Smithore, ©alvarez, Pg 4 ©mcpix, Pg 5, 9, 11, 13, 17, 18, 24, 28 ©MariatKary , Pg 6 ©By Igor Bulgarin, Pg 7 ©kali9, Pg 8 ©By lev radin, Pg 9 ©Justin Patterson Photography LLC, Pg 10 ©The Photo Access/Alamy Stock Photo, Pg 11 ©diego_cervo, Pg 12 ©MediaProduction, Pg 13 ©Gal Abahel, ©LuckyBusiness, ©wiki, ©fad1986, Pg 14 ©By Oleksandr Nagaiets, Pg 15 ©By Rawpixel.com, Pg 16 ©alvarez, Pg 17 ©Coast-to-Coast, Pg 18 ©deepblue4you, ©Ruthie Fierberg, Pg 19 ©vgajic, ©GoodLifeStudio, Pg 20 ©JackF, Pg 21 ©By Pavel L Photo and Video, Pg 22 ©KDPWWK, ©osker14, Pg 23 ©Nanette_Grebe, Pg 24 ©Ingram Publishing, Pg 25 ©Steve Debenport, Pg 26 ©FatCamera, Pg 27 ©Aksonov, Pg 28 ©Gal Abahel, Pg 29 ©Artranq,

Edited by: Keli Sipperley
Cover and Interior design by: Rhea Magaro-Wallace

Library of Congress PCN Data

A Dancer / Sandra Athans
(So You Wanna Be)
ISBN 978-1-64156-470-0 (hard cover)
ISBN 978-1-64156-596-7 (soft cover)
ISBN 978-1-64156-711-4 (e-Book)
Library of Congress Control Number: 2018930506

Rourke Educational Media
Printed in the United States of America,
North Mankato, Minnesota